A NOTE TO PARENTS

In *Bicycle for Sale*, Oswald learns a lesson about recycling. With some cleverness and elbow grease, he uses recycled objects to transform an old bike into a unique, personalized bicycle that he prefers over a brand-new one.

As you read, talk with your child about the transformation of Oswald's bike. For instance, ask your child what Oswald does after each friend comments about his bike. What objects would your child use to "fix" the bike? How does each alteration change the bike? Discuss ways your family participates in similar recycling—sharing hand-me-down clothes and toys or repainting and mending furniture rather than simply throwing it away.

Encourage your family to recycle. Make it an everyday occurrence that becomes a natural habit. Let your child help sort bottles, cans, and boxes, and talk about the personal and environmental benefits of reusing items and materials.

When you visit your local library or bookstore, select a few books on the environment. There are many titles that make learning about environmental issues interesting and fun.

Learning Fundamental: **science**

For more parent and kid-friendly activities, go to www.nickjr.com.

BICYCLE FOR SALE

Published by Scholastic Inc., 90 Old Sherman Turnpike, Danbury, CT 06816

SCHOLASTIC and associated logos are trademarks and/or registered trademarks of Scholastic Inc.

ISBN 0-7172-6619-2

Printed in the U.S.A.

First Scholastic Printing, September 2002

BICYCLE FOR SALE

by
Dan Yaccarino

illustrated by
Antoine Guilbaud

SCHOLASTIC INC.

New York   Toronto   London   Auckland   Sydney
Mexico City   New Delhi   Hong Kong   Buenos Aires

Oswald the octopus and his pet hot dog, Weenie, loved to ride by Bingo's Bicycle Shop and look at all the lovely new bicycles.

Johnny looked at the bicycle and declared,
"I would like to buy it, but the paint is peeling."

"That's true," Oswald agreed,
"it needs a fresh coat of paint."

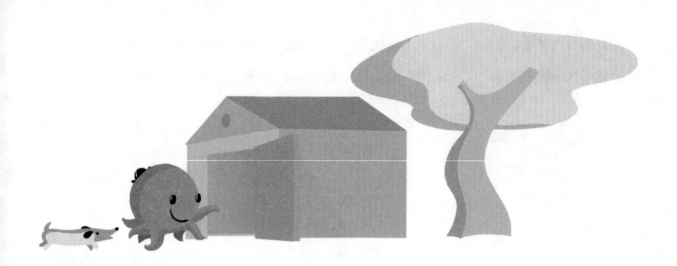

Oswald went to the backyard shed and found
a can of Blueberry Blue Super Gloss paint.

Then he and Weenie painted the bicycle.

After the paint dried, Daisy passed by.

"Hey, Oswald," she said, "I'd buy your bicycle, but the seat is torn."

"That's true," Oswald agreed, "it needs a new seat."

Oswald went to the kitchen and found a lovely turquoise tea cozy.

Then he and Weenie put it on the bicycle.

Madame Butterfly and her daughter, Catrina Caterpillar, came to look at the bicycle.

"Good afternoon, Oswald," said Madame Butterfly.

"Gubba gubba," said Catrina Caterpillar.

"I was looking for a new bicycle and would like to buy yours, but the tires look rather old," Madame Butterfly said.

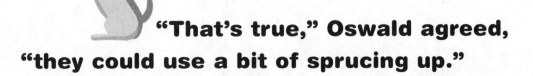

"That's true," Oswald agreed, "they could use a bit of sprucing up."

Oswald went to the backyard shed and found a can of Whipper Willow White paint.

Then he and Weenie painted new white walls on his old bicycle tires.

Henry walked up to the bicycle and looked at it very closely.

"I would buy your bicycle, old chum," Henry said, "but the chain is all rusty and dirty."

"That's true," Oswald agreed, "it could use some fresh oil."

Oswald went to the kitchen and got a bottle of Olivia's Olive Oil and poured it on the chain.

Then he and Weenie put it back on the bicycle.

Up strolled the Egg Twins, Egbert and his brother, Leo.

"Good day, Oswald!" said Egbert.
"Yes! Yes! Good day indeed!" said Leo.
They inspected the bicycle and tried the horn.
Wonk moaned the horn sadly.
"Hmm," said Egbert.
"Yes, yes, hmm," said Leo.

"We'd buy your bicycle," Egbert explained, "but it needs a new horn."

"Yes, yes," said Leo, "it sounds simply dreadful, old boy."

"That's true," Oswald agreed, "it needs a new horn."

Oswald went to Weenie's bed and found an old rubber bone that went *Toot! Toot!*

Then he and Weenie put it on the bicycle.

"That should do it, girl," said Oswald.

"It's got a fresh coat of paint, a new seat,
white wall tires, a shiny chain, and a new horn!"

He decided to ride his old bicycle to Bingo's Bicycle Shop to take another look at the new red bicycle in the window.

At Bingo's Bicycle Shop, Oswald and Weenie met a few friends.

"What a great new bicycle!" said Johnny Snowman.

"Why, thank you," Oswald said, "but this is my old bicycle. Weenie and I fixed it up all by ourselves."

"Wowie kazowie!" Daisy said. "It looks brand-new!"

"Quite stunning," Egbert said.

"Yes, yes," Leo agreed. "Quite."

"Weenie, you know what?" Oswald asked.
"I like my old bicycle just fine."

A little while later, Johnny Snowman strolled by.

"Why, hello, Oswald," said Johnny. "I see you're selling your bicycle."

Oswald parked his old bicycle in front of his building.

Then he painted a sign and hung it from the rear basket.

Oswald said to Weenie, "Girl, it's about time I buy a new bicycle and sell this old one. It has peeling paint, a torn seat, worn tires, a rusted chain, and a broken horn."

One day, they saw a beautiful new red
bicycle with a three-way adjustable
seat, white-wall tires, and a
glistening silver chain.

On the handlebar
was a bell that
made a wonderful
Zing! Zing! sound.

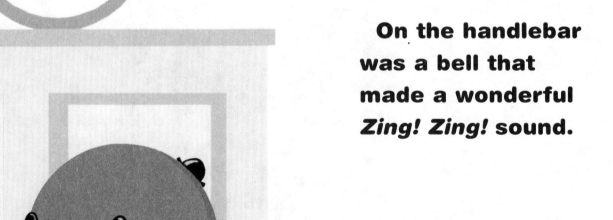